BAREFOOT BOOKS

The barefoot child symbolizes the human being whose natural integrity and capacity for action is unimpaired. In this spirit, Barefoot Books publishes new and traditional myths, legends, and fairy tales whose themes demonstrate the pitfalls and dangers that surround our passage through life; the qualities that are needed to face and overcome these dangers; and the equal importance of action and reflection in doing so. Our intention is to present stories from a wide range of cultures in such a way as to delight and inspire readers of all ages while honoring the tradition from which the story has been inherited.

SALT IS SWEETER
THAN GOLD

by Andrew Peters

Illustrations by Zdenka Kabátová-Táborská

BAREFOOT BOOKS

BOSTON & BATH

Barefoot Books, Inc.

the children's book division of

Shambhala Publications, Inc.

Horticultural Hall

300 Massachusetts Avenue

Boston, Massachusetts 02115

Graphic Design by Design/Section

Printed in Belgium by Proost International Book Production

This book has been printed on 100% acid-free paper

Peters, Andrew

Salt is sweeter than gold: a Czech folk tale/retold by Andrew Peters;

illustrations by Zdenka Kabátová-Taborská.

p. cm.

Summary: Insulted when his youngest daughter compares him to salt, the king banishes her
until he realizes the true meaning of what she said.

ISBN 1–56957–933–4

[1. Fairy tales. 2. Folklore, Czech.] I. Kabátová-Taborská, Zdenka, ill. II Title.

PZ8.P4425Sal 1994

398.21'09437—dc20

94–7672

CIP

AC

It is the custom in certain
parts of Moravia that when a guest
comes to your door you must offer
her bread and salt.

The king was growing old, so old that the wrinkles fell like waves down his face. Soon he would die. But how should he divide his kingdom among his three daughters? He thought deep and long about it. Then he came up with an answer. "I shall ask each one of my daughters who loves me the most, and she shall have the whole kingdom after I am gone! That is a very clever idea!"

So he summoned all his nobles and all whom he thought were his friends to a grand public ceremony. His three daughters came in and the eldest stepped forward, then went down on bended knee to speak. "Father, I love you more than all the jewels that encrust your fingers and all the gold that lies hidden down in the vaults of this castle!" She spoke as ungreedily as possible, and the king was well pleased with her answer.

Next, the second daughter stepped forward, then went down on bended knee to speak. "Father, I love you more than all the land that spreads like an ocean beyond this castle!" She too spoke as ungreedily as possible, and the king was well pleased with her answer.

Last, the youngest daughter stepped forward. She stood her ground and did not bend her knee. "Father, I love you more than salt," said she, who loved him truly.

"Salt, salt!" shouted the king, who was most insulted. "The day that salt becomes more precious than gold is that day you shall be my daughter once again! Leave this place in banishment, for you are no longer mine!" The king had spoken, rashly as usual, but his word was law.

So it was that the young princess left the castle
with only the clothes she was wearing.
Surrounding the castle, for it was a
long time ago, a great forest spread
to the horizon, and soon the princess
became lost. She was tired and her
heart was so heavy.

Where could she go?

As if in answer, a little path appeared in front of her. She followed it and the trees opened on to a clearing. In the middle stood a stone cottage. The cottage was well kept and surrounded by a vegetable garden. The girl went to knock at the door. As she did so, an old woman came out. This was Babichka, the wise one.

"I need rest for the night and food. Can you help me, dear lady?" asked the princess.

"You need more than rest, dear child. But can you cook, sow seeds, chop wood?" asked Babichka.

"I can do none of these things, but I am willing to learn." And so the girl was welcomed into the little cottage. As the days passed, she learned how to do things for herself rather than waiting for them to be done. The old woman was kind and soon the princess settled down, though she never forgot her father far away.

At the castle, the king was growing older still. Now, he had only two daughters to choose between. Soon he would have to make his decision. And there must be a feast! It would be a great feast. All the noblemen and courtiers of the realm would attend, so that none would forget the power the king held over the land. The invitations were sent out and a date set.

The day before the feast, there was a great thunderstorm, and it rained through that day into the night. Outside the king's castle, the geese stretched their necks up to the rain. Far away in the woods, Babichka smiled.

The next morning, all was busy down in the cavernous castle kitchens. The cook was chopping vegetables. He was as round as a ball, and many times larger, with a puffed white hat on top of which lived a chick. It was the safest place for the bird, and the cook fed her scraps. The cook looked at his pocket watch. The time had come to visit the salt and pepper cellars, and begin the seasoning of the dishes.

Off went the cook, down the steps to the cellars. Suddenly, there was a great scream that shook the walls of the castle. The cook squeezed his way up along the corridors, running through the castle to find the king. He burst into the royal boudoir. "Oh, most noble patron!" said the cook, frantically wiping the rivers of sweat from his brow. "All the salt has been washed away in the storm last night!"

16

The king was not too worried, but quickly sent winged messengers to the four corners of his kingdom to find some salt. Within the time it takes a heart to forget, the messengers returned with these words, "Your Majesty, what little salt there is is more precious than gold and none will part with it!"

Then the king remembered what he had said to his youngest daughter. But he was a king, and kings must not show their feelings. "So, cook of mine, make sweet dishes instead!" he commanded.

With this simple solution, the cook waddled back down to the kitchens to prepare the feast.

So the nobles came, and their families, their servants, their baggage and horses. Slowly the feasting room filled. At first, all was politeness, for the king was not a man to make an enemy of.

The people sat down. Steaming dishes were brought forth. Toasts were toasted. Forks were raised and the feast began. But at the first bite of the food, one after another of the nobles put down their forks in disgust.

"This is sweet!" they each screeched one by one, and one by one they rose up from their chairs. Without a word to the king, they gathered up their retinues and left.

The king could not believe his eyes. The great hall stood empty, apart from his two smiling daughters who had no complaint about the food. His heart was so heavy, it could crack. He would have cried, but tears have salt in them, so even they stayed stuck inside him. Soon he grew ill and had to be taken abed. The two daughters smiled even more and plotted quietly.

20

Far away in the forest, Babichka smiled also and addressed the young princess. "It is time for you to make your way back home, my lady! Your father is ill, and only you can help him. Take this," she said, and handed her a small black velvet bag. "It will help you on your journey. And when it is empty, remember to follow the wind over the three hills and through the three valleys. You will come to a grassy mound. Knock three times, and you shall see what you shall see!"

The princess took the bag and opened it, finding it full of salt. Although she did not understand, the girl said nothing, but kissed the wise woman on both cheeks and left without looking back. The forest no longer filled her with fear, for she now knew well its ways and wildness.

But by end of day, the princess was lost. Where could she go? As if in answer, a path appeared in front of her. She followed it to a poor-looking hovel. As she came to the door, a young man opened it. "I would welcome you in, my lady, but have no salt for the bread. It was all washed away in the great storm!" he said. In reply, the princess took her velvet bag of salt and sprinkled some on a piece of bread. All was well, and she found rest that night.

Day came again, as it always does, and the princess went on her way. But soon she became lost. She was tired and her heart was so heavy.  Would she ever find her way home, or even a place for the night? As if in answer, a little path appeared before her. She followed it and the trees opened on to a clearing. In the middle stood a fine merchant's house, made of good red brick. As she came to the door, a young man opened it: "I would welcome you in, my lady, but have no salt for the bread. It was all washed away in the great storm!" he said, before the princess could say anything. In reply, she took her velvet bag of salt and sprinkled some on a piece of bread. All was well, and she found rest that night.

Day came, as it always must. Word about the young woman with the bag of salt had spread through the forest, and now a throng of folk stood outside the house. None knew her for the princess, for she had changed inside and outside. As she left, thanking the young man for his courtesy, the crowd followed her.

This time she was not lost, but came by the middle of the day to the gates of the castle whence she had been banished. She knocked on the wooden door, saying to the guard in a quiet voice that she had a cure for the king. All remedies had been tried, and death was not far from the old man now. So the guard let her in, and a servant came to lead her through the corridors and up the stone stairs to the cold room in which her father lay.

The curtains were pulled back, and there lay her father, all shriveled up like a dried pea, his eyelids gummed close together. He could not see and asked who was there. In silence, the princess opened the velvet bag and took the last grains of salt to put them on her lips. Then she kissed her father on both eyes. As she did so, he began to cry and was able to see again.

"Daughter of mine, forgive me!" was all he could say. She smiled and joined with his crying, which soon turned to laughter, much to the annoyance of the two sisters who sat outside the door listening. But the bag was now empty! What had Babichka said?

"Father, I must leave you for a while, but this time I shall not be gone from your heart!" sang the girl, and she ran with the wind out of the castle, past the crowd, over the three hills and through the three valleys until she came at last to a grassy mound. She knocked three times and the mound opened like a door.

In front of her was a tunnel of ice, though it was not cold. She walked through it, and the tunnel grew into a cavern so deep she could not see its end. In the middle stood a garden of white roses. She bent to pluck one. As she did so, a few white grains dropped on to her hand. She licked her fingers: the rose was made of salt! Then she understood.

Now, two white stallions appeared, drawing a fine white carriage, fit for a queen. She stepped in and the horses galloped through the cavern, out of the tunnel, down the three valleys and over the three hills, until they arrived back at the castle courtyard.

Far away in the forest, Babichka smiled. There was a crack of thunder and the carriage, horses, bridles, bits, wheels, and spokes all dissolved into a mountain of salt on which sat the princess.

The king could now rest in peace. As for the two older daughters, they could not believe in such magic; such a shock it was that they both had heart attacks and died.

The mountain of salt was a throne, and the princess became known ever after as the Queen of Salt.